A CHILD'S BOOK OF POEMS
ALL THROUGH THE YEAR

A CHILD'S BOOK OF POEMS

ALL THROUGH THE YEAR

ILLUSTRATIONS BY
FRAN EVANS

Pont

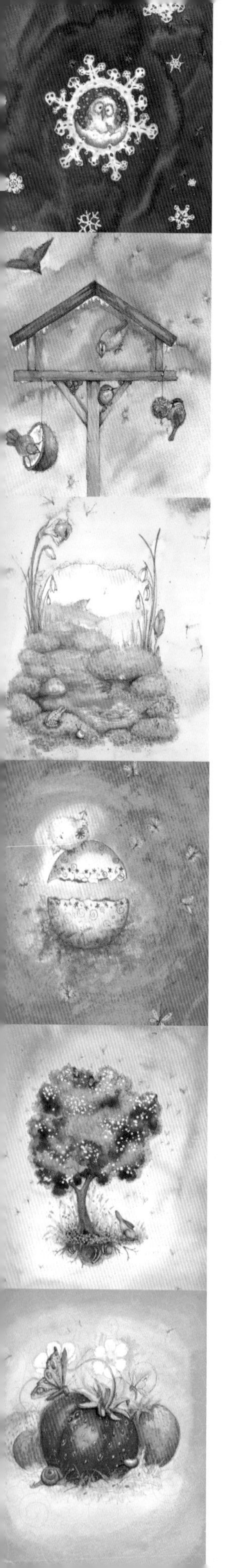

Contents

Introduction: A Poem a Day — 11
Gillian Clarke

JANUARY — 13
Catherine Fisher

FEBRUARY — 19
Phil Carradice

MARCH — 25
Francesca Kay

APRIL — 31
Chris Kinsey

MAY — 39
Gillian Clarke

JUNE — 45
Frances Thomas

JULY 53
Phil Carradice

AUGUST 59
Francesca Kay

SEPTEMBER 65
Catherine Fisher

OCTOBER 71
Chris Kinsey

NOVEMBER 81
Gillian Clarke

DECEMBER 87
Frances Thomas

A POEM A DAY

Read a poem every day.
They're short and made of lovely words,
friendly, small as little birds.
They're really easy to remember.
So January to December,
read a poem every day.

Sing a poem every day
to keep the boredom bug away,
and when you go out to play,
drum it, dance it, make it rhyme,
learn it off to pass the time.
Try a new one every day.

When you're lying in your bed
and you can't sleep, in your head
sing a verse or two instead
of counting sheep. To help your slumber
January to December,
see how many you remember.

Gillian Clarke

JANUARY

NEW YEAR ADVICE FROM AN OLD BOOK

For the first of the months is called Januarie
after the two-faced god,
who looks forward and back all at once.
On this day nothing, not even the smallest coin,
should leave your house.
Do not lend fuel, or matches, do not pay bills
or you will lack money all year.
Do no washing. Or one of your family
might well be washed away.

Get a dark-haired man to come to your door at midnight.
He must bear a coin and coals, or a fire.
He must bring food, and be fed.
You will have luck all year.

A warm Januarie means a sharp spring.
Frost in the fields, a fine harvest.
Send some careful person to the well
to draw the first water in silence.

Give to beggars, feed birds, warm your hands by the fire.
And on the coldest days, the shortest days,
wassail your apple trees and dream of summer,
Watch the lake turn to glass and slowly freeze
around the roots of your heart.

TWELFTH NIGHT

Take down the tree. Tuck its tinsel
away tidily, its baubles in boxes.
Carry the holly to the heap by the hedge.
Let the decorations fall from the ceiling
into their old folds. Roll up stockings,
pack santas, store the bent
drawing pins in their tiny white tin.
Carefully unplug the winking lights
that made the night magic. It's over now.
Blow out the candles round the crib,
put ox, Mary, shepherds, into their beds of straw.

But wait. There's still a star.
And three strangers are knocking at your door.
They hold gifts, they look a little weary.
What have you done with the infant King? they say.

SUN IN JANUARY

comes at you low
across the eyes,

all slants and angles.
Over car parks,

through the slit
between chapel and hill,

pale
and uninterested,

its glance sidelong,
its face turned away.

But each grass blade
has a long shadow,

and out from your feet
a giant spindles on snow,

its head in the far woods,
its arms wide as fields.

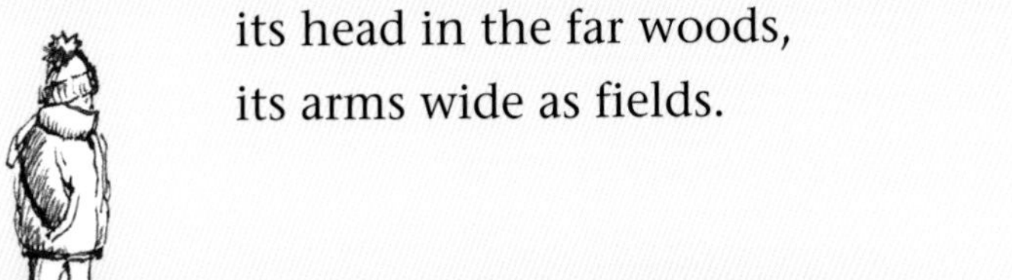

INVITATION

Mr and Mrs Frost and their son, Jack,
 are pleased to invite you
to their annual winter extravaganza
 in the house of January.

Dress code – gloves, boots,
 heavy coats and if you've got them, skates.
Underneath, secret as shivers,
 gowns of silver, suits of silk.

Come by sledge over the tundra,
 sleighs drawn by reindeer,
motorized skis, snow cats,
 huskied by a thunder of white bears.

You'll drink from crystal cups,
 eat from glass plates,
sorbets and ice cream and syllabub
 diamond-frosted, snow-sherded.

And all night you'll dance
 circles on the frozen floor;
while the world hibernates and the Northern Lights
 pick out your shadow.

Outside, a sliver of moon
 will wait to escort you home.
Your gift, a cloak of night,
 sequined with stars.

Catherine Fisher

FEBRUARY

THE MUD POOL

A wild weekend of February rain – floods surged
across the road onto our football field.
'Do not go near,' Miss Dawson urged. 'It's dangerous!'

But after school, once teachers left, we'd paddle off
to Timbuktu or China, places that we knew,
from geography, lay far across the sea.
'Wider than Lake Eyrie,' cried Danny Willett,
who was always reading. All week
we sailed our boats, cut channels in the mud.
No one waded through – though Tommy Bowen tried,
his boot-tops sunk, submerged, before he reached halfway.
His socks were brown as berries,
toes like wrinkled prunes, when he got back.

It could not last.
One night Tommy pushed in Millicent Jones.
She sliced the air like an Olympic diver
and bellyflopped with grace – then ran home, crying.
Next day Miss Dawson summoned us and while
she shouted, called us 'Fools!', a lorry came –
three men and a pump as noisy as Niagara.
Our pond was gone by lunchtime,
had flown away as quickly as it came.

For years, each winter, we waited,
willed it to return. It never did again.

SNOW

Snow that year,
snow so deep
it lay like icing on the hills
and fields of Wales.
Snow roller-coastered
down the sullen sky,
then fountained upwards,
like a geyser, from the ground.

Higher than our backyard wall,
higher than the window ledge,
the snow lay, bandaging the house.

Grumbling, Granddad cut steep steps
into the ice and we climbed out,
escaped our sudden igloo –
to freedom and the joy
of snow so deep we thought
that it would last forever.

FEBRUARY FOOTBALL

Freezing fingers,
Runny nose,
Legs all red,
Icy toes.

Stood in goal,
Face like ice,
To see the ball
Would be nice.

I've got a cold,
I'm feeling sick,
I swish at nettles
With a stick.

I hate PE,
I'm really bored –
Was that the ball?
It was. They've scored.

STRENGTH IN WINTER YET

A February day
As cold and grey as slate.
White horses in the bay,
A mass of foaming hate.

Hills black against the sky
Like rows of sleeping kings,
Geese calling as they fly
In wind that roars and sings.

Sharp rain-squalls beat at houses,
The town is soaking wet.
The world turns over, rouses,
There's strength in winter yet.

Phil Carradice

MARCH

AT LAST

No stopping it
as buds swell and soften
the silhouettes of trees

no stopping it
as the birds sing of
each day lasting a little longer

no stopping it
as the air, though cold and grey,
now tastes fresh and new

no stopping it,
the spring at last,
and the garden is waking

frost grips the soil
but snowdrops burst through

nothing holds them back,
those first small drops
in the great spring flood that
sweeps away the winter.

BREAKFAST

A hedgehog woke from hibernation,
Shook the spikes upon his back.
'I wonder if the worms have woken up,' he said.
'I could do with a little snack!'

I WISH I WAS A TADPOLE

I wish I was a tadpole,
Wriggling my tail,
Dashing in the water,
Pretending I'm a whale.

I'd splash around quite happily,
Swimming all the day,
Wriggling my little tail,
And with my friends I'd play.

I'd grow some legs and shed my tail,
And turn into a frog,
So I could hop as well as swim,
And sit upon a log, saying:

'Ribbit, ribbit, ribbit!'

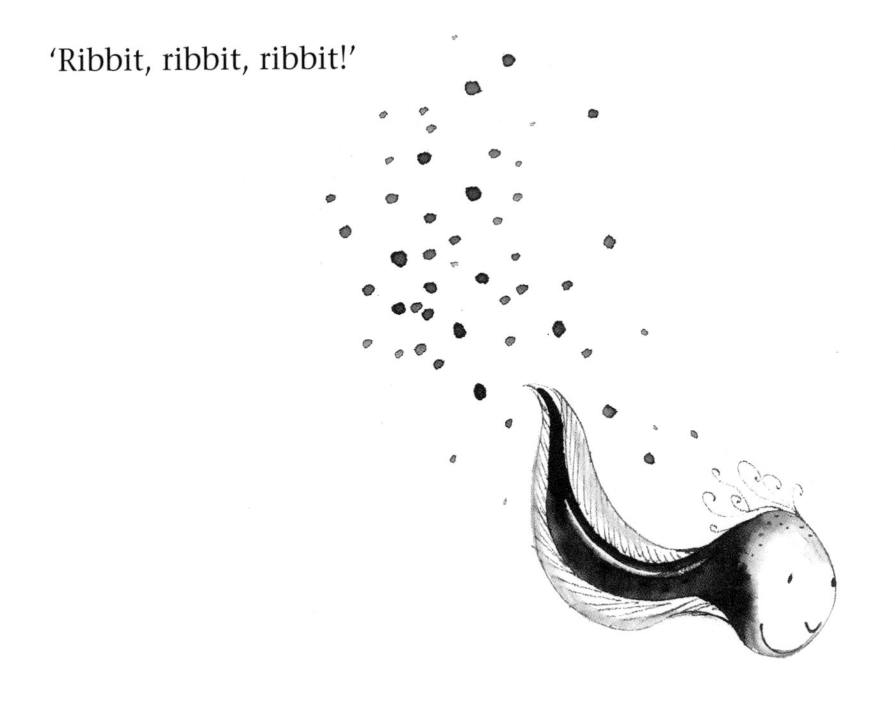

THE SPRING SUN

It shines on flowers
That smile so sweet,
And on dancing daffodils.

It shines on spreading fields of grass,
On tall mountains and
On smaller hills.

It shines on lambs who skip and call,
On fluttering birds who tweet and sing,
And long thin worms who slowly crawl,
It shines on every living thing.

The sun so warm,
It makes life grow,
Looking down on earth below, and saying,
'Here comes spring!'

Francesca Kay

APRIL

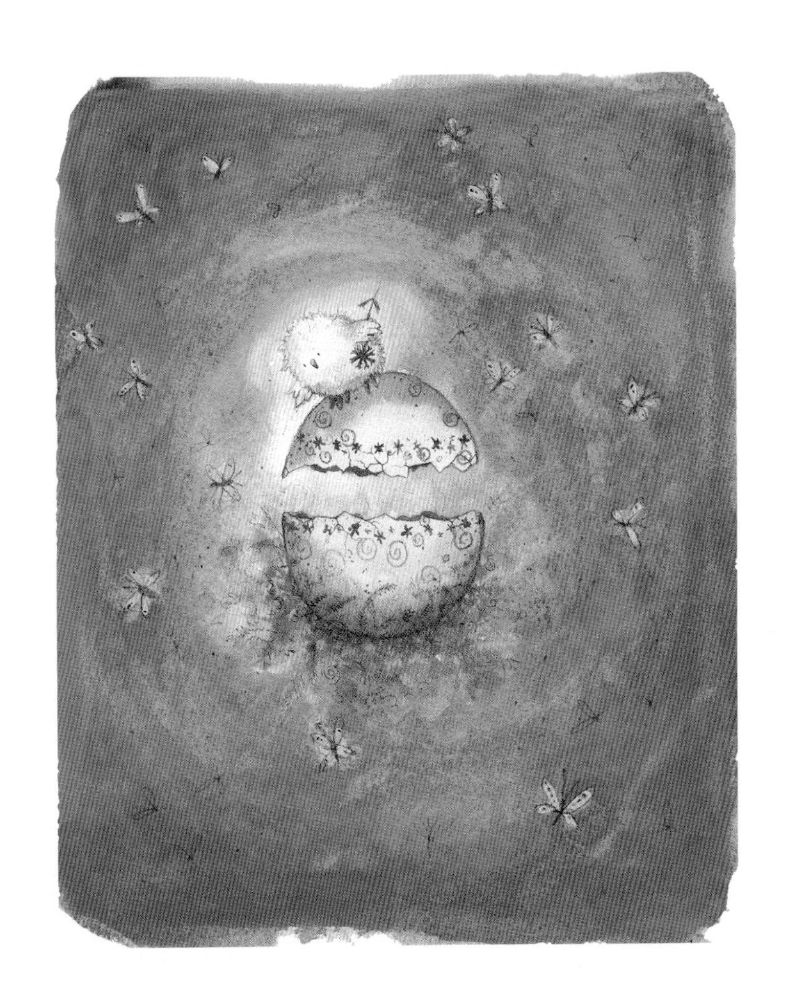

WHAT HAPPENS TO THE APRIL FOOL?

All jokes must stop at midday on 1 April

It's not fair! It's not fair!
I'll play my pranks with the weather,
I'm trickster to sun, clouds and wind.

I'll coax out the sun like a new balloon,
rub him warm and set him to shine.
You'll all shed your coats and I'll grab mine.

With my cloak of cloud, I'll cover the sun,
smother all warmth and light,
send you from sweat to a shiver.

I'll hurl rain hard and straight at the ground
or send it in sideways, slant and slashing,
and set the windscreen wipers dashing.

I'll cast my raindrops into the jet stream,
they'll come back as frozen marbles, then it's hail,
all hail, the world goes pale, and tongues

start poking and sucking, trying, and failing,
to taste gobstoppers made of ice.
After the mush, the slush and the squish,

put on your wellies to splat, splash and splish
and I'll round it off with a rainbow.

RIVER TREASURES

Silver, emerald and gold.
Silver, emerald and gold.
A river in April can make you feel bold
but it protects its treasures
by being cold, cold, cold.

The shallows may sing,
Come on in. Come on in.
But they'll chuckle if you buckle
and swallow you down,
sweep you off to drown, drown, drown.

So stay on the bank under the willows
and watch yellow ducklings fluffing the currents.
When they're riding the rapids their mothers go wild
and herd them to calm, to eat and to preen
in the still water that is green, green, green.

Silver, emerald and gold.
Silver, emerald and gold.
A river in April can make you feel bold
but it protects its treasures
by being, cold, cold, cold.

Stand where the current looks softer or still
and spy out an island all scattered in gold.
Midas's kingcups are thriving on silt.
Here, the problem's not what you think,
it's one of sink, sink, sink.

Silver, emerald and gold.
Silver, emerald and gold.
A river in April can make you feel bold
but it protects its treasures
by being cold, cold, cold.

MIGRATIONS

Say goodbye to white-fronted and barnacle geese
wearing the motley colours of snow-thaw.
Listen for trumpeting, the last of the whooper swan,
whose parting wingbeats swish like slides of melting snow.
They aim for the Arctic and nest-sites way up north.

Watch the skies and see
specks, arrowheads and trailing tails.
Swallows and martins fly from the equator,
pause on power lines then catapult
to acrobatics in air and scooping up mud for a nest.

Soon the swifts will boomerang back, skimming for flies.
They sound like fairground screamers
waltzing around your chimney pots.
Let them in, let them in, to holes in your walls,
crevices in rocks. The only time they rest
is when they nest.

RISING TIDE

Wade into woodland, wait a while there.
Let a horse-chestnut tree overtake you,
feel the force of bud breaking leaf.

Walk through the white foam of wild garlic
and the blizzard of the cherry tree,
stand in curling waves of bluebells.

Become part of a land tide:
the surge towards summer is on.

Chris Kinsey

MAY

NEWT

Secretive amphibian
in the night garden,
she lurks in her stone den,
or hunkers under the coal
so you'll never tell
where her nest is hidden.

But on a May night
search the pond
by torchlight
for the little moon-bright
dinosaur
in her lair.

Little dragon
of the garden,
asleep at noon,
she's up late stitching a cot
to a leaf of water-crowfoot
by the light of the moon.

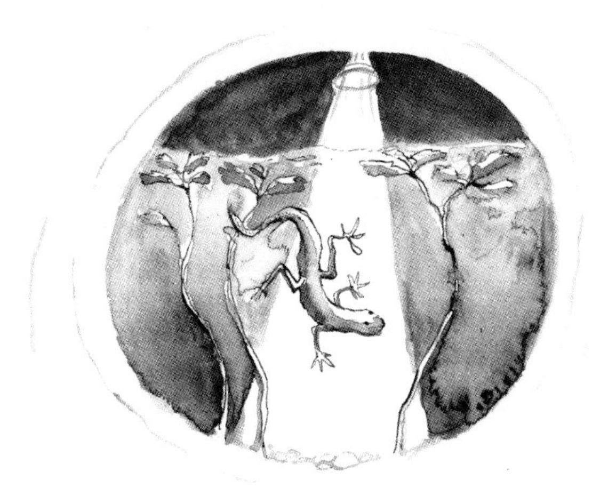

A GIRL CALLED NIAMH

Niamh, Niamh,
rhymes with Eve,
heart-on-her sleeve
and semibreve.

One May eve
in the apple-blossom trees
she played her flute
to Adam and Eve.

'Eve, never leave him,
never deceive him,'
sang Niamh in the garden
of make-believe.

But Eve was aggrieved
and Adam was peeved,
ate the apple she thieved,
felt completely deceived.

'Not my fault!' he grieved.
'It was her!' 'Better leave,'
said God, and they went,
with never a by-your-leave,

leaving Niamh,
sweet and naïve,
to retrieve
the apple-core chucked in the trees.

THE HAND-GLASS

Look through the lens
at the palm of your hand
and bring to mind
what is too small to see:

a spiral of weightless stuff
like the house of a wasp,
but microscopically small, husk
no air is thin enough to thread.

And it turns out to be
the cast-off skin of a green-fly,
that, being made of star-dust,
knows all about galaxies.

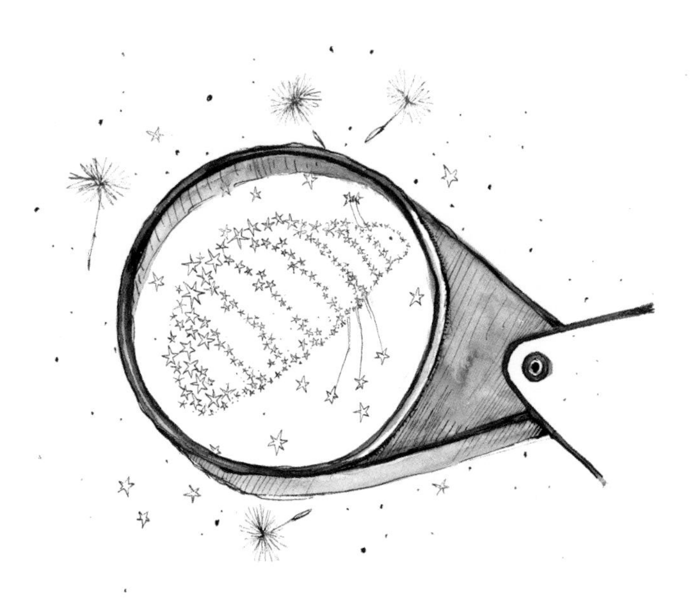

BLACKBIRD

Blackbird in the chestnut tree
before the sun is up
wakes me up at half past three
with a brimming golden cup.

Blackbird sings six syllables,
flute and whistle in one,
over and over, silver bells
awake the rising sun.

Blackbird sings in summer rain,
sleek and debonair,
takes a sip and sings again
in the blue-green air

Blackbird's eye is a gold ring.
His beak is full of gold,
and all he has to say and sing
is the oldest story told.

Blackbird's eye is a wedding ring
he brings his mate in May,
and all the summer hours he sings,
and sings the dark away.

Gillian Clarke

JUNE

MIDSUMMER

Midsummer's magic they say
And it's true;
With the sweet scent of roses
All the day through.

Parties in gardens
And bikes in the park;
Even at bedtime
It never gets dark.

Cricket bats thwacking,
Oh what a catch!
Tennis at Wimbledon
Game, set and match.

Sun cream and ice cream,
Strawberries for tea:
Midsummer magic
Is working for me!

GRASS

Here come the lawnmowers,
Strimmers and shears,
Edgers and hedgers,
Buzzing and fierce.

Cut it down! Cut it down!
Make it all flat.
What grass should be like
Is a green velvet mat.

But go to a meadow
Humming with bees,
Where the wind softly brushes
The tops of the trees.

And the grass grows unnoticed,
Feathery-free,
In a silvery drift.
Just stand there and see . . .

Rye grass and oat grass
Sway in the breeze,
Timothy grass,
Like a soldier at ease,

Quaking grass shivering
As you go past,
Fescue and woodrush
And sweet vernal grass.

Millet, and marram
That grows in the dune,
Cord-grass, and couch grass
Foxtail and brome . . .

Long grass a-shimmer
Like waves of the sea,
Secret and silent . . .
Just stand there and see.

BIRD CHASES CAT

Small bird – swift, delicate, airy;
Large cat – Rosie, ruthless hunter.

Nest under the eaves,
Fledglings twittering,
Mother Swift fussing.

Rosie comes stalking,
Considers leaping,
Scattering nest and nestlings,
Imagines cat triumph!

But Mother Swift's ready, and
SWOOSH!
Down dives like a missile,
Swoosh! And again!

Rosie stops, startled.
And again! Again! More!
Small bird skimming sleek fur.

Cat flinches, bewildered
and runs,
twitching her tail.

CUCKOO

'In April I open my bill,
In May I sing night and day,
In June I change my tune,
In July away I fly,
In August leave I must.'

Traditional rhyme

I wish I knew, cuckoo-bird,
Why you sing two:
Cuck-cuck and *oo*.

Next month you'll leave us,
Far, far you'll fly;
Is this your way
Of saying goodbye?

Frances Thomas

JULY

JULY, THE END OF SCHOOL

Six whole weeks ahead of me:
The beach is fun, it's cool,
Seaweed, sand and castles –
July, the end of school.

Dappled sun on pavements,
Light till ten at night.
July's the time for barbecues –
Summer's at its height.

Running through the cornfield,
Building hides and dens,
July's the very best of months –
Just hope it never ends.

SPORTS DAY

It's end of term, it's Sports Day,
I'm running round the field.
My T-shirt flaps about my knees,
I'm trying to win the shield.

The trouble is I'm just no good
At sports and games and stuff.
The high jump's hard – and throwing, too,
And running's really tough.

I'd rather lie out on the grass
And watch the clouds float by.
Or walk upon a golden beach,
So glad that it's July.

But better here than sat in class,
The sun upon my back,
And as the swallows swoop and dive
I lumber round the track.

In time, maybe, I'll win a race –
The cat that got the cream.
Till then I'll just enjoy the day,
Quite happy with my dream.

THE HERON

All morning, under summer sun,
the heron stands
on matchstick legs, waiting,
patient as a judge,
beside the rock,
out in the stream, eyes fixed,
all senses focussed.

Soft ripples mark
the surface of the water –
his prey is coming.
The sun is strong,
but the heron doesn't notice:
his mind is on the kill.

One dart, one diving dash –
it's over. And now the heron stands
once more, his feathers
wet and dripping from the stream:

Ready to strike again.

SUMMER STORM

The night the storm came,
dragons roared
outside our window;
their breath –
bright lightning flashes –
forked the far horizon.
The old house trembled,
flinching
under each and every bang.

'Come on,' said Dad
and led us to the garden.
We sat on the veranda,
gasping as the rain fell
in torrents like a waterfall.

'Remember this,' Dad said,
'it's nature at her best.'
We sat on in the rain.
Thunder crashed
and Dad was never closer
as summer slipped
between my fingers.

The night the storm came
and dragons roared
outside our window.

Phil Carradice

AUGUST

IN TOWN

It's an ice-cream summer,
A dusty backyard summer,
A hot pavement summer,
A finding some shade summer.

It's a sun-cream summer,
A paddling-pool summer,
A bare-feet summer,
A late-to-bed summer.

It's a peaches-and-cream summer,
A slow, lazy summer,
A windows-open summer,
A never-sitting-indoors summer.

It's a summer we'll remember,
And think it was always
Just like this.

IT'S A GOOD IDEA

strawberry
vanilla
mint chocolate chip

in the heat
they squish and drip

ice cream
doesn't like the sun

melted ice cream
isn't fun

now, my friends
here's an idea
wait until the winter's here

in the winter's
snow and ice

ice cream won't melt.
Oh, very nice!

ON THE BEACH

sharp mountains
dividing sea and sky

a line of sailboats
obedient to the wind

a row of seagulls
perched on the rocks

tiny ripples
reaching the shore

neatly placed sunbeds
slumbering in rows

everything so perfect
on the beach.

HIGH TIDE

The fields are flooded with sunshine,
It swirls through parched corn,
Washes over dusty hedgerows,
Drenches weary trees,
Dripping into trembling shade.

A tide of heat drowns the land,
Every living thing submerged,
Slow and breathless in the golden ocean.

There is nothing to do but wait,
Wait for the tide turning,
And the slow ripples of night.

Francesca Kay

SEPTEMBER

FIRST DAY OF TERM

The school wakes. Listens.
Someone's unlocking its chains.

A bird flies up from its roof.
Spider webs break in a draught.

The school uncurls, interested.
Its heart starts to thud.

The blinds of its eyes roll open.
Its doors yawn.

The school stretches. The school purrs.
Voices rumour in its corridors.

In the staffroom machines chunter.
A waft of coffee wanders.

The school is hungry. It's been a long summer.
Loud and urgent, its bell summons.

All around, from streets and roads and cars,
children sleepwalk into its jaws.

BLACKBERRYING

There are trains on the embankment. Stop and watch.
They clank above the brambles
where you're purpled, pipped, scratched, itched.

Your fingers are sore, your jumper's skagged. You struggle;
but the juiciest leave just stains,
the best always too high, too far. You wriggle,

squash, trample. Plump wet ones
come apart in your fingers.
Small dry berries are solid as stones.

Crisp beetles drop on you, wasps dart. Spiders
run round in a hurry, sewing up holes in their dreams.
You're all tangled, your sleeves, your hair,

snared in a mesh-world of squirms,
blood-sucked thumbs, scratches and sneezes,
harvest heavy in your arms. September.

Berries in a basket, sun-slant in your eyes.
Take it home. Eat it. Bake it in pies.

SEVEN SWANS

Seven swans
fly over the house,
in close formation,
heading south,

their wings are white,
necks outstretched,
eyes intent
on the sky's edge.

I'll rise from my bed.
I'll pull on my shoes.
I'll follow the swans.
As poets do.

AUTUMN

High in his tower the wizard stews his spell.
He uses rain and bees and spider webs.
Compost and mulch. Smoke from a hundred allotments.
Fungi from the deep wet woods.

Every year the wizard adds some extras.
The sound of a footstep striding across the stubble.
Sand from a child's abandoned bucket.
An old woman's song. A schoolboy's yawn.

Things ending, decaying, finishing, gone.
All the yellows and ochres and reds in the world.
Zigzags of gnats. The very last swallow.
Apples and pears and berries and sloes and haws.

The wizard stirs his season. Above his tower
the stars are summoned to watch.
Pegasus the horse, Andromeda the princess;
the small bright glitter of the Pleiades.

In the cauldron are the colours of autumn.
Tonight he'll go out and paint each tree.
You'll know he's been when your foot crunches
the first dead leaf on your path.

Catherine Fisher

OCTOBER

OH, O, OCTOBER

Oh, O, October,
the year is getting older
and leaf colours are bolder.

Hazels drop jackpots of gold.
Oak trees bronze and throw down acorns,
Beeches cast coppers and hard spiky masts,
Cherry trees set sail in bright crimson boats.
Horse chestnuts spread yellow fingers
but have to let go.

Blackthorns blaze, leaving bitter purple sloes,
Hawthorns shrivel and shed red waxy berries,
Maples' broad palms hold out for more light,
Ashes keep keys in clusters like jailers.
Sycamores scrabble, dotty with tar-spots.
Silver birches fountain molten gold.

Oh, O, October,
is the time of exposure,
when winds get colder.

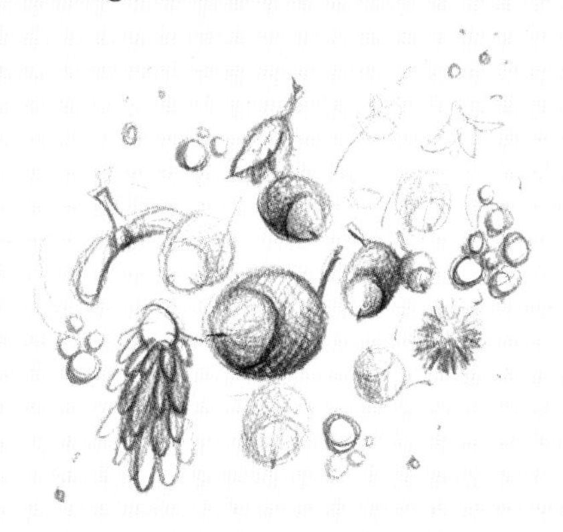

WHO STOLE THE LEAVES?

Who stole the leaves?
'Not me,' said the sun.
'I, I, I make them come!'

Who stole the leaves?

'Don't point at me,' said the frost.
'I just coat them in crystals
and sparkle a change.'

Who stole the leaves?

What about rain?
'Not I,' said the rain. 'I'm with the sun –
tree roots soak me up and turn me to sap.'

Who stole the leaves?

'It's you! It's you!' They picked on the wind.
Wind looked worried, then said,
'I just help them along. They're willing to come.'

Who stole the leaves?

'Hush,' said the tree.
'Why don't you ask me?'

Who stole the leaves?
'Me!
I shut each one down and let it go free.

I'm better off bare
when winter winds blow,
safer as sticks when storms sweep through.

And, as for snow,
my poor leaves would catch it
and hang me down low.

So, in October
I start my great treasure race.
Anyone, everyone, can share in the chase.'

FUNGI HALLOWEEN

It's a Halloween Party, come warts an' all.
No one will ask if you're wearing a mask.
Sick green skin? Come on in.

Deathly pale – you'll not fail.
Shrivelled, brown and bald? Or blushing
with a zit? You'll certainly fit.

But, beware,
this do isn't about 'trick or treat',
it's all about 'dare'!

Come on down to the graveyard,
feel the face of a headstone,
touch what's engraved there.

Trace the scale of lichens,
sink into a cushion of moss,
probe the lobes of liverwort.

Look deep into cracks and spy
fronds of rustyback and spleenwort,
a woodlouse ghosting away.

Feeling bold?
Then follow the trail of poisonous yew
to the woods as the light's getting low.

By the light of chanterelle torches,
and bulbs of sulphur tuft,
dodge splodges of orange-peel fungus

to seek out the sickener and death cap.
Meet the pure white destroying angel,
and scarlet fly agaric, but don't touch . . .

and definitely, definitely, don't taste!

JACK O'LANTERN

Put a face on a pumpkin.

Snip him from his stem,
cut the top off his head.

Scoop the seeds from inside,
hollow out the pulp.

Slice a smile or slash a scowl,
sculpt some jaggedy teeth.

Blinkety-wink, poke out two eyes.
What do you think?

Flicker-licker, install a candle
and light up the wick.

Flicker-licker, breather of fire.
Set up your doorstep defender.

Your gatepost gurner will out-grin
the darkness . . .
till the candle goes out.

OCTOBRRR

Brrr to the blackbirds staking out roosts
Brrr to robins bobbing between berries
Brrr to last butterflies braving late ivy.

Say a long goodnight to the hedgehog.
He'll not be scuffling and snuffling for slugs
but heading to curl in dry leaves.

Say goodbye to the skimming bats,
no more sky-skating round street lights
for they hang themselves up in caves and hollows.

Say au revoir to amphibians and reptiles
as they slither and burrow underground.
It's too brrr for them so they hibrrrrnate.

Chris Kinsey

NOVEMBER

REMEMBER, REMEMBER

Pile on one three-legged chair.
And another, look, a pair.
Kitchen table, missing drawer,
worm-eaten dresser, broken door.
A worn-out yard-brush with no bristles.
A barrow-load of stalks and thistles.
Six assorted cardboard boxes,
oranges, apples, Bramleys, Coxes.
The dog's old basket. A wooden tray.
An old bale of mouldy hay.

One match to set newspaper curling,
a slash of magazines unfurling.
Whoosh, a roar, a tower of fire
and all is blazing higher, higher.
Rockets flower in the dark
and fall to earth in golden sparks
to cries of oooooh and aaaaah, and then,
'We never want tonight to end.'
The bonfire dies and falls apart,
and leaves its embers in your heart.

STORM

The cat lies low, too scared
to cross the garden.

For two days we are bowed
by a whiplash of hurricane.

The hill's a wind-harp.
Our bones are flutes of ice.

The heart drums in its small room
and the river rattles its pebbles.

Thistlefields are comb-and-paper
whisperings of syllable and bone

till no word's left
but thud and rumble of

something with hooves or wheels,
something breathing too hard.

ONE DAY IN NOVEMBER . . .

our kitchen went missing,
six cupboards, five doors,
four drawer fronts, three drawers,
scarpered, gone, disappeared.

There were not enough hinges
and too many whinges
and no one in IKEA
had the foggiest idea

till Beverley Everleigh
ever so cleverly,
beavering steadily
beat the bureaucracy

found what went missing
in the dungeons and doldrums,
amid grumbles and tantrums
in the mystery land of IKEA.

But Beverley Everleigh
human and friendly,
found what was lost
in Glasgow or Paisley,

and before we went crazy
that lady, not lazy,
arranged the delivery
and a big van brought us the lot.

MY BOX

My box is made of golden oak,
my lover's gift to me.
He fitted hinges and a lock
of brass and a bright key.
He made it out of winter nights,
sanded and oiled and planed,
engraved inside the heavy lid
in brass, a golden tree.

In my box are twelve black books
where I have written down
how we have sanded, oiled and planed,
planted a garden, built a wall,
seen jays and goldcrests, rare red kites,
found the wild heartsease, drilled a well,
harvested apples and words and days
and planted a golden tree.

On an open shelf I keep my box.
Its key is in the lock.
I leave it there for you to read,
or them, when we are dead,
how everything is slowly made,
how slowly things made me,
a tree, a lover, words, a box,
books and a golden tree.

Gillian Clarke

DECEMBER

BARN OWL IN WINTER

Wintry owl
Swoop like a ghost,
With your pale, painted feathers
Alight on a post.

Searching the darkness,
The grass white with frost,
Then downwards you plunge,
And a tiny life lost.

Hunting seems cruel –
But cruelty unplanned
Is taking your hunting ground,
Lays waste your land.

THE FOX OF MAIDEN LANE

It was late one cold December;
There were bottles of champagne,
And girls in party dresses
As we came out in Maiden Lane.

Now, Maiden Lane's in London;
There's not a blade of grass.
It was then we saw him stalking,
Alert, as bold as brass,

With his ginger-biscuit coat
And his eyes as bright as steel,
He sauntered through the dustbins,
Sussing out his evening meal.

He didn't heed the revellers,
Or mind the traffic's din,
He was calm, and cool and comfortable:
The Lane belonged to him!

We long ago left London,
Now home's a Radnor hill,
And foxes aren't our best of friends
For the chickens that they kill.

But I often think about him,
In my mind I see him plain
And I hope he lived for years and years
That fox of Maiden Lane.

THE UNIMAGINABLE

Of course I'd read about it, and wondered how it was,
But how to believe in it,
As heat shimmered on dusty roads,
And mangoes shone golden from dark leaves?

Then when we came to Cardiff
There was rain, certainly; a lot of rain.
And, no, they said, haven't seen it for years. Don't get it often now.
I thought, maybe it was a fairy tale,
Like giants and dragons and those
Things that lived in the hills.
Easier to believe in *them*!

Then one morning, when I woke,
No cars, no birds,
A soft muffled silence, and a strange light.
And my mother came in smiling.
'Look,' she said, and I looked . . .

And it swirled and fell from the sky like feathers,
Just as they'd said in the stories,
And made a new landscape of my road and my garden,
Whiter than anything, whiter than the whitest flower,
Than seashells, than doves,
And it clung to the wires like cotton wool
And spun spindles of white on the trees,
And gathered in drifts by the wall,
And a black cat walked right through it,
Daintily lifting her paws,
And I knew then that it was real.

MIDWINTER

I love midwinter,
The shortest day,
Curtains drawn close
And the world shut away.

Foxes prowl softly,
Pad through the snow.
Stars shine like diamonds,
Street lamps aglow.

Carols and candles
And holly for cheer,
Christmas is coming:
Best day of the year!

Frances Thomas

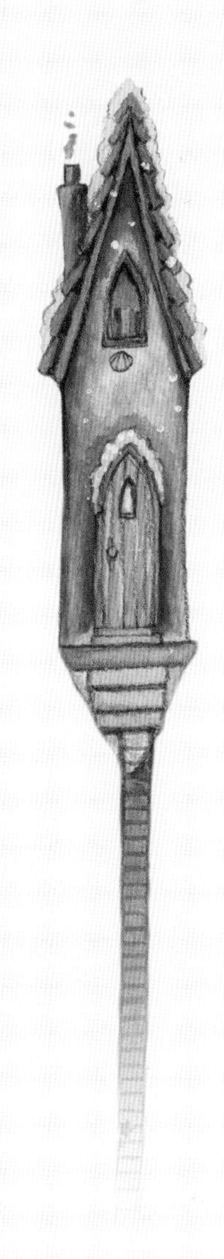

Published in 2010 by Pont Books, an imprint of
Gomer Press, Llandysul, Ceredigion, SA44 4JL
www.gomer.co.uk

ISBN 978 1 84851 166 8

A CIP record for this title is available from the British Library.

This volume is published with the financial support of the Welsh Books Council.

Printed and bound in Wales at
Gomer Press, Llandysul, Ceredigion SA44 4JL